MYTHICAL CREATURES

IN FOLK TALES FROM AROUND THE WORLD

RETOLD BY FIONA WATERS

ILLUSTRATED BY LIZ PYLE

Belitha Press

First published in the UK in 2002 by

Belitha Press Ltd
A member of **Chrysalis** Books plc
64 Brewery Road
London N7 9NT

ISBN 1 84138 318 X

British Library Cataloguing in Publication Data for
this book is available from the British Library.

Editor: Russell Mclean
Series editor: Mary-Jane Wilkins
Designer: Sarah Goodwin
Illustrator: Liz Pyle

Printed in Taiwan

10 9 8 7 6 5 4 3 2 1

CONTENTS

For Donald, who is one, and Helen,
with much love - F.W.

For George and
Ned with love - L.P.

VASILISA OF THE GOLDEN BRAID

THE TSAR SVETOZAR HAD TWO SONS and a daughter. I cannot tell you the names of the two brothers but they have only a small part to play here, for this is the story of their sister, Vasilisa of the Golden Braid.

The Tsar was determined to make a good marriage for his daughter and so, from the moment she was born, he had her locked in a small room, right at the top of a very tall tower, where only her ladies-in-waiting were allowed to set eyes on her. But it is difficult to keep such a secret, especially when the secret is very beautiful. Vasilisa was indeed outstandingly beautiful. Her corn-coloured hair fell to her feet like a waterfall of silk, and her eyes were the deepest green.

When she was twenty, her father the Tsar sent his ambassador to kingdoms that he wished to make alliances with. In his luggage, the ambassador carried a portrait of Vasilisa, and before very long royal suitors were arriving at the palace, impatient to see whether Vasilisa was truly as beautiful as the artist had painted her. Vasilisa was delighted at the prospect of being released from the tower at last. She plaited her hair into one shining long braid and demanded that her father let her outside so she might smell the fresh air and walk barefoot on the grass just for once on her own. He agreed, reluctantly, on the day of the great feast when she was to be married to one of the noble suitors.

But Vasilisa had *Just* scarcely set foot outside the tower when a huge whirlwind gusted out of the sky and swept her up so she was soon out of sight. The wind carried her far over mountains, plains and wide rivers and ~~deposited~~ *dropped* her in the kingdom of a fierce dragon who had heard of the great beauty of Vasilisa of the Golden Braid.

The Tsar was beside himself with rage. All his plans for his kingdom were at risk. The Tsarina wept for her lovely daughter. Her brothers swore undying revenge and set off to find Vasilisa.

They travelled through many lands, and after a year and a day they found themselves standing before a great golden palace. A sweeping staircase rose to the front door, which had a huge dragon's head knocker set in the middle. You can imagine their delight when they saw Vasilisa looking through the bars of one of the windows. The brothers ran up the staircase and struck the knocker loudly. The sound boomed round the courtyard as, very slowly, an ancient servant pulled the door open a fraction. Pushing him aside, the brothers rushed in, calling out:

'Vasilisa, where are you? We have come to rescue you!'

But it was not as simple as that. When they found Vasilisa they were shocked by her appearance. She was pale and thin, and her golden braid had lost its shine.

'My brothers, we must flee!' she cried. 'This palace is owned by a terrible dragon, and he will kill us all if he finds us here. He wants to marry me, but so far I have managed to put him off.'

No sooner were the words out of her mouth than they heard a rushing sound and the walls of the palace began to glow red with heat.

'It is the dragon! He is back,' cried Vasilisa. 'You must hide quickly.'

But the brothers refused to cower in a cupboard and so when the dragon flew in the door, he found two strange young men beside Vasilisa.

'Who are you, and what do you want with my Vasilisa?' he roared.

'*Your* Vasilisa?' spluttered the brothers. 'She is our Vasilisa and we have come to take her home.'

'Oh, is that how it is,' laughed the dragon, and he picked up the two brothers with his huge wings and threw them into the next kingdom. So that was the end of them.

Vasilisa burst into tears, and refused to eat or drink for days on end. Then she pulled herself together and began to think how she might best save herself. She decided to be kind to the dragon and so lure him into a false sense of security. She soon discovered that the only person the dragon feared was a brave hero called Ivan the Pea. His name sounded too much like a joke and so Vasilisa resigned herself to a life with the dragon, far away from her home. But as it turned out, the dragon was right to fear Ivan the Pea.

Back home, the Tsarina decided she must have lost all her children now, as her two sons had failed to return from their quest for Vasilisa. Her heart was heavy, and she never smiled. One day she was walking in the garden with her ladies-in-waiting. It was stiflingly hot and when they came to a small pool, the Tsarina asked for a cup of water. She did not notice as she swallowed the icy-cold water that a tiny pea lay at the bottom of the cup, and so she swallowed that, too.

Some months later, to her great astonishment, the Tsarina gave birth to a son. He was very round and jolly and she called him Ivan the Pea. He grew at a prodigious rate, and when he was only ten he was already a powerful warrior. One day the Tsarina told him the sad tale of his brothers and his beautiful sister, Vasilisa of the Golden Braid. Of course, Ivan immediately wanted to go in search of them, but the Tsar forbade it in case he too never returned. But Ivan begged and begged so much that in the end the Tsar gave him his blessing and sent him on his way. The Tsarina wept for her youngest son.

Ivan travelled with a light heart. He had journeyed for many moons when he came one evening upon a curious little house in the middle of a dark forest. It was made of wood and stood upon a chicken leg. As Ivan drew closer, the chicken leg turned round and there sitting in the doorway was a truly ancient woman. Her face was deeply lined and her straggly grey hair was tied in an untidy knot. She had not a single tooth in her head.

'Good evening, Babushka,' said Ivan politely. 'Did you see a whirlwind pass this way ten years ago carrying a beautiful girl with a long golden braid?'

'Alas, young man, I know all about your whirlwind. It is no wind but a terrible dragon who has your beautiful girl. His palace is not far from here, and I can certainly tell you how to find it. But you must first go to visit the blacksmith and ask him to make you an iron staff that no man but you will be able to lift, for only such a weapon can crack the skull of this dragon.'

So Ivan went the next morning to the blacksmith and told him to make the iron staff. All that day and the next, the blacksmith's forge glowed red and sparks flew high in the sky as he hammered and fashioned the staff. When it was ready, it took ten men to lift it, but Ivan picked it up and tossed it into the air and then caught it again with just one hand.

'It is a fine staff, thank you,' he said to the blacksmith and returned to the curious little house in the middle of the dark forest, standing upon a chicken leg, where the old woman was waiting for him.

'Now, you must undertake one more thing,' said the old woman. 'You must promise to bring me some water from the fountain in the courtyard.'

'A little water is easy to bring,' promised Ivan.

'But this is no ordinary water,' said the old woman. 'This water will make me young again.'

'I shall bring you your water, I promise,' said Ivan, 'and then perhaps I shall marry you, Babushka!'

The old woman cackled with laughter, and then rose stiffly to fetch supper for Ivan.

The next morning, she told him to follow the sun until it set, when he would be at the edge of the forest that surrounded the dragon's golden palace. Ivan set off with a glad heart, and a renewed promise to bring the old woman her water from the fountain in the courtyard. It was as she had promised. Just as the sun was setting, its last rays caught the gleam of the golden palace. Ivan wrapped himself in his bearskin cloak and slept peacefully under a huge tree until dawn. He watched the golden palace carefully until he saw the terrible dragon fly up in the sky and far off to the mountains where he would spend the day hunting.

Ivan strolled up to the palace where he spotted Vasilisa peeping out of her window.

'Good day to you, Vasilisa of the Golden Braid. Will you let me in, please?' called Ivan. 'I am your brother, and I have come to rescue you.'

'Alas, I have no brothers, they were killed by the dragon many years ago,' replied Vasilisa. 'But what is your name?'

'I am called Ivan the Pea, and I am your brother. Let me in, please,' said Ivan.

Vasilisa sped down the stairs. But the dragon had bound the great door with the dragon's head knocker fast with many bolts and chains, and she could not open it.

'Stand back!' ordered Ivan, and with one swipe of his hand the door crashed to the floor. Ivan stepped over it carefully, and bowed to Vasilisa.

'My dear sister, you are as beautiful as our mother the Tsarina told me.' This was not quite true, for Vasilisa was a pale shadow of her former self, but it pleased her greatly. And she was even happier when Ivan explained that he truly was her brother.

'Can it be that you are Ivan the Pea, the only man in the world that the dragon fears?' she asked, her heart beating furiously.

'I am called Ivan the Pea,' said Ivan, 'but I don't know if the dragon fears me. I certainly don't fear him,' he said boldly and sat down on the dragon's great iron bound chair. It shattered into a thousand pieces under him.

'Oh dear,' said Vasilisa, 'you have broken the dragon's favourite chair. Now he will know you were here.'

'He will certainly know I am here. I will be waiting for him when he returns,' smiled Ivan. And he persuaded Vasilisa to come with him for a picnic in the forest while they waited for the dragon to come home. Towards evening, they heard a rushing sound like a mighty whirlwind.

'It is the dragon!' cried Vasilisa.

Ivan pushed her gently but firmly under the trees and told her to stay hidden. Then he walked swiftly to the sweeping staircase rising to the front door, with the huge dragon's head knocker set in the middle, and there he waited for the dragon.

Soon a dark shape appeared on the skyline, and with a sweep of his wings, the dragon landed by Ivan. He was a very terrible dragon. He had the body of a gigantic snake, covered in scales like a fish, and cruel talons curled at the ends of his massive webbed feet. His great flapping wings were black as a midnight bat, and his spiked tail swished from side to side in anger. His enormous head was topped with sharp horns and two rows of pointed teeth gleamed in his slavering jaws. Smoke curled from two flaring red nostrils, and he looked very bad-tempered.

'Ah hah!' he roared, and the ground trembled at the sound, 'I see the great Ivan the Pea has come to fight me. Well, I am frightened of no man,' he bellowed and he raised one of his massive webbed feet to crush Ivan. But Ivan was having none of that. He side stepped, and brought his huge iron staff crashing down on the dragon's head. And that, quite simply, was the end of the dragon.

Ivan helped Vasilisa out from under the trees, and showed her the body of the dragon so she might really believe that she was free. Together they found the fountain in the courtyard, and filled a flagon with the magic water. Then they mounted one of the dragon's fleetest horses and galloped as fast as they could away from the dragon's palace.

They stopped at the curious little house in the middle of the dark forest standing upon a chicken leg, and gave the old woman her bottle of magic water, thanking her for all her help. Then they galloped again as fast as they could through day and night, and eventually arrived home. The Tsar and Tsarina were overjoyed to see them both safe and sound again. The celebrations lasted for many days and nights, and everyone lived happily ever after. Ivan the Pea grew up into an even mightier warrior, but he always looked after his sister, Vasilisa of the Golden Braid.

THE DEATH OF THE CHIMAERA

THE KING OF LYCIA, IOBATES, was greatly troubled. Lycia was under siege, but not by an invading army or a mighty warrior, but by a fearful beast called the Chimaera. This beast was the sister of Cerberus, the terrible three-headed dog who guarded the underworld. The Chimaera was an awesome creature. She had a lion's head, a goat's body and a serpent's tail. The lion's head spouted fire like a dragon, the goat's body could twist and turn with great agility, while the serpent's tail was armed with fierce spikes that could shoot poison into an enemy at one hundred paces. Many brave heroes had died trying to defeat the Chimaera, and it seemed she was impossible to kill. Iobates despaired. Vast tracts of his country were being destroyed by the beast, houses were burnt down and the people fled in terror.

Then Bellerophon arrived at the court. He had been sent by Proetus, King of Argus, who was married to Iobates' daughter, Anteia. The foolish Anteia had fallen in love with Bellerophon, who was indeed a handsome and proud young man. But Bellerophon was also an honourable young man, and so when he recognized Anteia's admiration, he refused to speak to her or even to sit in the same room as her.

Spurned love quickly turns to hatred, and so Anteia told her husband that Bellerophon had tried to kiss her, quite the opposite of the truth. Proetus was naturally very angry, and sent Bellerophon to Iobates with a sealed letter, telling him what Anteia claimed and asking Iobates to put Bellerophon to death immediately. But Iobates found Bellerophon to be a courteous young man, and he was reluctant to do as Proetus wished. Then he thought of a splendid plan. He would ask Bellerophon to kill the Chimaera and thus might solve both his problems at one blow.

Bellerophon, of course, was delighted to be given such an undertaking and went to the temple of the goddess Athene to ask her advice. In a dream that night, Athene appeared and told him that the only way he might succeed would be if he could tame the fabulous flying horse, Pegasus. Athene placed a golden bridle in Bellerophon's hands, adding that only with this bridle could the horse be captured.

When Bellerophon awoke the next morning, the golden bridle was clasped firmly in his hands and so he offered a prayer of thanks to Athene and set off to catch Pegasus. He knew that the great creature stopped every day to drink from the enchanted pool on Mount Helicon, and so he found a shady place under an olive tree beside the pool and sat and waited. Before long Bellerophon heard the beating of great wings, and then Pegasus glided into view and landed by the pool. He was a magnificent beast. He was pure white and huge, with great sweeping wings tipped with silver and a flowing, glistening mane. He snorted when he saw Bellerophon and pawed the ground. But Bellerophon spoke softly to him, and came up close enough to slip the bridle over his great head.

Pegasus stamped in dismay at the touch of the bridle, but the touch of Athene was obviously still there, for he soon let Bellerophon sit on his broad back, and the two of them flew high into the sky.

While they flew, Bellerophon talked soothingly to Pegasus and told the noble horse all about the terrible Chimaera, and how they would defeat her. They flew over green fields and olive groves, over sparkling rivers and vines laden with grapes. But soon the landscape changed. It was like flying over a barren waste. Everything was burnt and charred, trees, crops and even houses. Not a living soul was to be seen, and smoke hung heavy over everything.

Pegasus flew lower and Bellerophon looked down, seeking the dreaded Chimaera. Pegasus neighed wildly, his teeth bared as he craned his long neck from side to side. And then with one dreadful bound there she stood! She was a horrifying sight. Foul fumes and black smoke issued from her mouth. She flexed her talons, and her lethal tail swished from side to side. Bellerophon gripped Pegasus with his knees, and strung his bow. Arrow after arrow he let fly at the Chimaera, but still she roared her defiance. Pegasus had to swoop and bank steeply to avoid her fire-laden breath, but he never faltered for a moment.

The battle raged for hours, and Bellerophon could see that the Chimaera was tiring. Pegasus took him even lower and with a mighty thrust, Bellerophon plunged a spear deep into the Chimaera's gaping mouth. At the end of the spear, Bellerophon had set a lump of lead, and as the fire rose in the Chimaera's mouth the lead melted and flowed down her throat and into her stomach. With a final fierce bellow of pain, the Chimaera rolled over and died.

Pegasus soared high up in the sky and whinnied his triumph. So Lycia was freed of its terrible scourge. Great was the rejoicing and Iobates welcomed Bellerophon back with gladness in his heart. During the great feast Iobates had arranged to celebrate Bellerophon's victory he showed the young man the letter Proetus had sent.

Bellerophon was able to explain what had really happened, and Iobates promptly offered his second daughter's hand in marriage to Bellerophon. And they should all have lived in great happiness ever after, but Bellerophon was a proud young man, and he grew to be an arrogant young man as more and more praise was heaped on his head for defeating the Chimaera.

He forgot the debt he owed to Athene. He forgot the part played by Pegasus. He grew quite insufferable. In his pride he even began to think he was an equal to any of the Gods, and one fateful day he decided to ride Pegasus all the way to Mount Olympus, the Gods' earthly home. Up, up they rose, Bellerophon crowing in triumph. But Zeus, King of all the Gods, looked on this with growing anger.

He sent a tiny gadfly to bite Pegasus, who reared up in surprise. Bellerophon slipped off his back and tumbled all the way back down to earth, and so that was the end of him. Pegasus flew on to Mount Olympus and was welcomed by Zeus, and to this day he carries thunderbolts for the greatest of all the Gods.

THE GREAT GIANT KINAK

IRELAQ THE HUNTER WAS OLD AND TIRED, and this made him grumpy. He would shout at his dogs when he thought they were not running fast enough. He would shout at his wife, Tutlik, if she did not have his meal ready when he came in hungry from hunting. He knew he was grumpy and he knew he was not kind to his wife, but he could not help himself.

One night he was especially angry. He tossed a seal he had caught on to the table and ordered his wife to cut it up without so much as a please or thank you. Tutlik silently cut up the seal, and rolled the skin into a small bundle which she placed on the table. Then she turned to go outside, telling Irelaq that she was going to wash her hands in the snow. And it was a very long time indeed before he was to see her again.

Tutlik walked and walked. All she wanted to do was to put as many footprints between her and her grumpy husband as she could manage. She walked and walked through the winter nights and she kept going north. It grew colder and colder but still Tutlik walked on.

Soon she had left all the villages far behind and there was only endless snow, as far as the eye could see. Now the cold was intense and Tutlik realized she needed to rest. But where was she to find shelter?

She knew if she merely stopped in the snow, she would sink into a sleep she would never wake from. Peering into the distance, she thought she saw a distant hill that seemed to have five peaks to it. On she struggled and when she was closer it crossed her mind that the hill looked just like an enormous foot. But she climbed over the first of the five peaks, and sweeping the snow away, she lay down in the gap between the two and was soon fast asleep. Tutlik slept for three days and three nights, and then, greatly refreshed, she went on her way again.

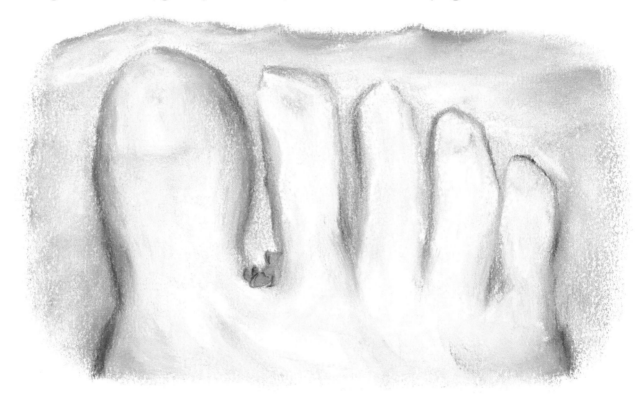

She walked the length of a long ridge and when she reached a gentle hill she rested again. It crossed her mind that the gentle hill looked just like an enormous knee. Tutlik set off again and the next night she sheltered in a shallow depression in the middle of a smooth plain. It crossed her mind that the shallow depression looked just like an enormous navel. She slept very well and the next day she walked and walked a very long way. When she came to a small valley, she decided to rest there and so she curled up in a great thicket of brushwood without another thought, and fell fast asleep.

When she awoke, she stretched and was just about to start walking again when a huge voice boomed out,

'And who might you be?'

Tutlik was absolutely terrified. She looked all round but could see no-one. The voice came again, and this time it was gentler.

'Why are you here? No-one has ever been to see me before.'

Tutlik looked all round again, but still she could see no-one. But she thought she had better reply so, trembling from head to toe, she told the unseen person that she had run away from her husband because he was always so cross. She explained that she did not know where she was going, nor indeed did she know where she was. The booming voice laughed, and it was a happy sound.

'Well, I can tell you the answer to your last question. You are sitting just between my nose and my upper lip, and I caution you to move away for if I breathe too hard I will blow you away.'

Tutlik was sitting on top of the great giant Kinak. She had been travelling along his huge body ever since she slept between the two peaks of the hill that looked like an enormous foot. It *was* an enormous foot!

The voice boomed out again.

'You must be very hungry. I will give you something to eat,' and a huge black shape moved over Tutlik. It was Kinak's hand, and it dropped an Arctic hare at her feet. Tutlik moved away from the small valley that was Kinak's chin, made herself a fire and cooked the hare and ate it all up. She felt very much better after that. Then suddenly Kinak said to her,

'Quick, you must find a place to hide – I am going to sneeze!'

She had no sooner scrambled down into the giant's tangled beard than with a great bellow, the giant Kinak sneezed the snow all over the place. Tutlik could see that there were certain disadvantages to living on top of a giant. So she looked around and decided that she would be safest to the left of his nose

and there she built a small shelter. Every day, Kinak's huge hand would hover over Tutlik and then some creature for her next meal would land at her feet. Not only was she well fed, but she had soon replaced her travel-stained clothes with new ones made from the skins of the animals so generously given to her by Kinak. Of course she did not use them all so before long she had a valuable collection of fine skins.

There came a day when Kinak asked her if she wanted to go home again and visit her people.

'I am very stiff from lying in the same position, so I want to turn over. If you were still here I might crush you,' said Kinak.

'I would like that very much,' replied Tutlik, 'but I am afraid of my husband. I left home because he treated me so badly.'

'You need never fear him again,' boomed Kinak. 'I will send you home, and should you ever need me all you have to do is call, "Kinak, Kinak, help me!" and I will be there.' So Tutlik began to make her preparations to go home, thinking that it would be a long journey. But Kinak laughed at her.

'You do not need to walk all that long way back, I can send you there very much faster! But first you must cut all the ear tips from the skins you have collected and put them in your jacket. Then you must stand in front of my mouth,' he said.

Tutlik did as she was bid, and Kinak began to blow, very gently, through his mouth. Tutlik was picked up and carried far over the snow until she landed right outside her old home in the village. And all round her, on the ground, lay heaps and heaps of valuable skins and furs. Every single ear tip had turned into a full-size skin!

Tutlik stamped the snow from her boots and went inside. Irelaq was very pleased to see her for he had found he missed her. And he was even more pleased when he saw the huge pile of skins and furs. He promised he would treat Tutlik better in future. Soon the couple were the wealthiest people in the village, and there was plenty of food on the table. It did not take Irelaq long, however, to revert to his old ways and he became grumpy again. Tutlik was having none of it. She called to Kinak.

'Kinak, Kinak, help me!' and the words had scarcely left her lips when an icy wind blew through the house. It blew Irelaq out of the door and away down the path leading out of the village, and Tutlik never saw him again. She never saw the great giant Kinak again, either, but she knew he would always protect her. Sometimes when there was an especially fierce and cold blast of snow-laden wind she would smile to herself and say,

'There he goes sneezing again. How glad I am to be in my warm home, and not sleeping under his nose!'

THE OLD TROLL
OF BIG MOUNTAIN

LIFE WAS VERY DIFFICULT for the poor old farmer and his wife. They had nothing much more in the world than their tiny tumbledown cottage on the edge of the dark forest, their two goats and their precious son, Olle. Olle was the apple of their eye because he had come to the old couple very late in life and so they felt doubly blessed. He was a cheerful boy, but a complete innocent and this always worried his mother.

The farmer and his wife scratched out a living on a poor field that was some distance from the tumbledown cottage. Every morning they gave Olle some bread and a cup of delicious goat's milk. They would put the goats outside to graze, and then they locked the door to the tumbledown cottage and put the key under the big stone by the front door.

Olle's mother always told him not to let anyone in while they were gone, but truth to tell no-one ever came through the dark forest. Gossip had it that a big old troll had been seen at dusk one evening, shambling through the trees, and that was enough to keep people away.

Now one night when the farmer and his wife came home, weary from digging the stony ground in their little field, they discovered to their utter dismay that both their goats were missing.

'It will have been that bad old troll, you mark my words,'

25

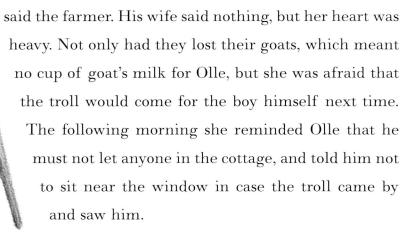

said the farmer. His wife said nothing, but her heart was heavy. Not only had they lost their goats, which meant no cup of goat's milk for Olle, but she was afraid that the troll would come for the boy himself next time. The following morning she reminded Olle that he must not let anyone in the cottage, and told him not to sit near the window in case the troll came by and saw him.

'And if that bad old troll does knock on the door, you must call out "Father, father, there is someone at the door," and that might scare the troll away,' she said.

'But how will I know it is the troll?' asked Olle. 'What does he look like?'

So his father sat him down and told him to listen carefully.

'That bad old troll is really, really ugly,' said his father. 'He has a huge mouth that stretches from ear to ear, he has a nose like a turnip, and he has a wolf's paw instead of a left hand. He has great big hairy feet, and he smells dreadful.'

Well, Olle did not think he could make any mistake about that, but just to be sure, he promised yet again that he would never open the cottage door.

So the farmer and his wife set off for their field again, locking the door behind them, and putting the key under the big stone. Once they had gone, Olle decided that he would make himself a big club so, if the troll was foolish enough to try to put him in a sack and carry him away to his mountain lair, he could biff him with the club. He looked around the cottage and found an old stick that his father had used to hold the window open in the summer. And then he looked around again, and found a rusty old fork that his mother had thrown into the back of a cupboard. So Olle tied the fork to the stick with the rope that had been used to tie up the goats. He was very pleased with his club, and twirled it round and round a few times to see how it felt, then propped it up against the door.

Now it was indeed the bad old troll who had taken the goats, and it was not long before he came back to the cottage to see what else he could find. He wasn't sure if there was anyone in and so he knocked on the door.

'Father, father, there is someone at the door,' called out the obedient Olle, and the bad old troll shambled back into the forest rather quickly. When his parents came home that night, Olle showed them his club and also told them that someone had knocked at the door. His mother was terrified, but his father was very pleased that Olle had done as he was told.

But the next day the bad old troll was back. He knocked on the door and this time when Olle called out,

'Father, father, there is someone at the door,' the bad old troll put on a big smile so that his great mouth stretched from ear to ear and looked in through the window.

'Hello,' said Olle. 'What are you looking in my window for?'

Well, the bad old troll could hardly say he was looking for a little boy to steal so he smiled an even bigger smile and said,

'Hello, Olle. I am looking for my knife which has fallen out of my pocket. Can you come and help me?'

'I'm very sorry,' said Olle, 'but my mother and father have locked me in so the bad old troll won't get me.'

'The bad old troll, eh?' said the bad old troll. 'Well, I don't look like a bad old troll do I?' and he laughed a big bad old troll laugh, but, of course, Olle didn't know that.

'No,' said Olle. 'I'm not afraid of you,' looking at the big smile. 'And I'm not afraid of the big bad troll either for I have my club here and I will biff that bad old troll if he tries to steal me.'

The bad old troll peered in through the window.

'I can't really see your club properly. Can I come inside and have a look?' he asked.

'Of course you can,' said Olle, all his mother's warnings flying straight out of his head. 'The key is under the big stone by the door.'

And before you could say 'never let anyone in' the bad old troll was inside the tumbledown cottage. Olle proudly showed him his club, but the bad old troll was itching to pop him in his sack and take him away, so he wasn't really listening. Olle wondered briefly why there was suddenly such a strange smell in the cottage, but he was too busy twirling his club around to pay much attention.

'So you see, when that bad old troll comes I shall be ready for him,' said Olle proudly.

'Well,' said the bad old troll, 'perhaps we could look for him together. I know where he hides his goats. If you come with me into the forest I could show you.'

'Oh yes please!' shouted Olle. 'I really do miss my cup of goat's milk every morning,' and he picked up his club ready to go. The bad old troll wondered whether he should just stuff Olle into his sack then and there, but then thought that if Olle was prepared to walk why should he carry him? Olle put some bread in his pocket and off the two of them went.

Olle reached out up take his new friend's hand, but the bad old troll looked shifty and said,

'You must take my right hand. I have hurt this one,' and he held up his left hand which had a big bandage wrapped round it.

'Oh, you poor thing,' said Olle, all his father's warnings about wolf's paws far from his mind as he took the bad old troll's right hand. And so they walked a little deeper into the dark forest. Before long Olle felt he would like a rest and so he sat down and took out his bread.

'Would you like some of my bread?' he asked the bad old troll.

'Certainly not,' shouted the bad old troll rather loudly, for of course trolls cannot accept anything from humans. If they do they are quite unable to behave in the proper troll manner, and all the bad old troll wanted to do was get Olle into his sack as soon as possible. Actually, he was rather annoyed that Olle was not at all frightened of him. It was always more fun when his victims were kicking and screaming.

'Olle, just suppose I was the bad old troll, what would you do?' said the bad old troll slyly.

But Olle just laughed.

'You couldn't be the bad old troll. You don't look anything like him, you just look like a poor old man. You can't fool me!'

The bad old troll thought this was very funny so he put back his head and roared with laughter. And as he did, Olle popped a piece of bread into that bad old troll's mouth! Well, he coughed and spluttered, and jumped up and down but he could not prevent the bread from slipping down his throat.

Now the tables were turned! The bad old troll found he could not even think of putting Olle into his sack, and he certainly couldn't take him away to his cave in the dark forest.

He took a small whistle out of his pocket and played a cheerful tune. Olle's feet tapped to the notes, but stopped as he heard a strange pattering sound. And then, out of the dark forest, came skipping his parent's two goats. Behind them trotted a whole herd of tiny kids, running and butting each other.

'Those are my parent's goats,' Olle exclaimed to the bad old troll. 'How did you find them so quickly?'

'Trolls have better ways of looking after goats,' the bad old troll muttered. 'Now you had better go back home before your mother gets worried,' and that bad old troll actually patted Olle on the head before turning back towards the dark forest. Olle called the goats to his side and went home, delighted with his efforts.

You can imagine his parents' astonishment when they came home to see not only their two original goats, but the herd of tiny kids as well. Olle told them the whole story from beginning to end. His father frowned, and then grew very cross.

His mother wrung her hands and began to shake from head to toe.

'So you see, he couldn't have been the bad old troll, could he?' said Olle happily. 'He had a big mouth from ear to ear, but he was very smiley. And his nose was not so very like a turnip, and I didn't look at his feet. And he certainly didn't have a wolf's paw for a left hand for his hand was all bandaged where he had hurt himself.'

His mother slid to the floor in a dead faint, and his father leapt to his feet.

'THAT WAS THE BAD OLD TROLL, YOU FOOLISH BOY!' roared his father, pulling out his hair. 'What did we tell you about never, ever opening the door?'

Olle could not see what all the fuss was about. He had brought the goats back home after all, hadn't he? But his mother and father never, ever left him alone again in the cottage. In any case the bad old troll was so embarrassed that he never, ever came near the tumbledown cottage on the edge of the forest again either.

THE PEDLAR'S SON AND THE GENIE

WALI THE PEDLAR HAD TRAVELLED far across the desert, and he was so very tired that he just let his camel take him where she would. He was so far from anywhere that he feared he was lost. Night falls suddenly in the desert, so Wali was relieved when the clever camel led him to an oasis with a well under swaying palm trees. The night sky glittered with endless stars, and the water from the well was clear and sparkling. Wali drank deeply and gave a bucket to his camel. He spread a threadbare carpet on the sand, wrapped himself in his robes and watched the moon rise.

'Most wise and excellent beast,' Wali addressed the camel as she sank to her knees, 'a thousand blessings upon your superior nose. What a haven of tranquillity you have led me to. I wonder to whom it belongs.'

No sooner were the words out of his mouth than there was a tremendous clap of thunder and a gigantic head appeared out of the well. Below a vast purple turban scowled a terrible looking Genie, and he was clearly displeased.

'Snivelling and impertinent mortal, I am the Genie of the Well and this is my oasis. How dare you drink my water without permission?'

The terrified Wali bowed low, and murmured, 'Ten thousand pardons, most magnificent Genie. I shall depart immediately.'

'I did not say you could leave! You have sullied my well by drinking from it and you must be punished,' roared the Genie. Wali was quaking in his sandals, but he faced the Genie bravely.

'Of course, O fearsome one. I shall do whatever you ask.'

The Genie looked somewhat mollified, but his words were uncompromising.

'You must give me whatever it is that your wife first hands to you when you return home, and this you must do without fail.'

Well, Wali heaved a great sigh of relief. His wife always brought him a glass of cooling sherbet when she saw him approaching.

'Ask and it is yours, O Genie. But how shall I find you again?'

'Have no fear, foolish mortal, I will present myself at your house five moons from now,' hissed the Genie, and slipped back into the well with a splash.

To his surprise Wali then fell fast asleep, and when he awoke in the morning he was inclined to think the whole thing had been a bad dream. Perhaps he had eaten too much goat's cheese before going to sleep. He roused his camel, who was not in a good mood, so she spat and shied as he put the great leather saddle on her back. All this put the Genie to the back of his mind as he turned towards home.

After a particularly trying journey, Wali was overjoyed to see his wife running to meet him. But his heart was gripped by a sudden fear as she thrust a small bundle into his arms, a joyous smile on her face.

'A thousand welcomes, Beloved Husband. Great has been my impatience waiting for you to return. See what Allah has sent us in his infinite mercy!'

Wali was speechless with despair as he looked down at his longed-for newborn son. Now he knew the Genie had been no dream, but a very real threat. When he told his wife what had happened on the journey she gave a shriek of despair, snatched the baby and held him tightly in her arms. They walked indoors slowly, terrified by the ill omen that suddenly hung over their heads. But Wali's wife, whose name was Noora, was a woman of great resolve, and before long her courage was restored.

'My husband, we shall defeat this wicked old Genie. We must seek to protect our son so no evil shall touch him.'

So Wali went to the Wise Man of the village, taking his tiny son with him. The Wise Man heard him out and then prayed for a long time before turning towards Wali with a gentle smile.

'I can protect your son, but you must do everything as I say. You must call him Ramadan, for he was born during the month of fasting, and this special name will be a protection to him. I shall give you a talisman to place round his neck. He must never take this off and so will be protected wherever he is and whatever he is doing.'

The Wise Man wrote a verse of the Koran in fine script upon a silver coin, and placed it in a leather pouch strung on a silver chain. He looped the chain round Ramadan's neck and put a hand on his head in blessing.

Time passed and Ramadan grew up to be a bold boy who played and scrapped with his friends in the dusty streets of the city. One day, the Genie of the Well suddenly appeared. The other boys fled at the sight of the Genie, but Ramadan stood his ground.

'Ah ha! Pedlar's son, I have come to take you away with me as that perfidious man, your father, promised me many years ago. I can give you a good life in a remote oasis, far away from all this noise and dust,' said the Genie.

'No, thank you very much,' said Ramadan. 'I like the dusty streets, all my friends are here. Whatever would I do in a remote oasis?'

And as he spoke a sneaky breeze blew open his jacket, so the Genie could see his holy talisman. He gave a snort of fury and disappeared as suddenly as he had arrived. Ramadan sped home, and told his parents about his encounter.

'Perhaps that will impress on you that you must never, ever remove your talisman,' scolded Wali. But Noora just checked that the silver chain was still securely fastened round Ramadan's neck.

Many years passed and Ramadan grew into manhood. He joined the army in the service of his king and travelled many lands in his service. Then a neighbouring king declared war, and Ramadan went into battle. The fighting was long and all the soldiers grew battle weary.

One night the enemy mounted an attack when everybody was sleeping. Around him, Ramadan's fellow soldiers were killed one by one, and he found himself surrounded. He said a quick prayer to his parents and turned to face his death. But suddenly there was a tremendous clap of thunder and the Genie of the Well appeared. He lifted Ramadan with one huge hand and clasped him to his chest. The enemy soldiers fled in terror.

'Noble Genie, a thousand thanks for saving me,' exclaimed Ramadan.

'Don't imagine that I was thinking of your worthless soul,' laughed the Genie. 'I was just looking after my property. One day I shall have you!'

The words were no sooner out of his mouth than there was a blinding flash, and there stood Suliman, Son of David. The Genie threw himself to the ground.

'Well you might grovel there, ignoble Genie,' thundered Suliman. 'How dare you threaten this young man. Know, brave Ramadan, that this Genie was condemned to live in the well as a punishment for his past wickedness. But in saving your life, a mortal life, he is pardoned and he now may join the good Jinns who guard my throne. Go, Ramadan, and live your life in peace.'

Both the Genie and Suliman vanished before Ramadan's astonished eyes.

Ramadan survived the war and when he eventually reached home once more he was able to tell the long-suffering Noora that his life was no longer in danger. They all lived long and contented lives. Wali, it must be added, was always very careful when he came to drink water from a well.

NEPHELE AND THE UNICORN

SEVERE THE HUNTER HAD SPENT a very successful day in the forest. His game bag was full of pheasants, and his arrows almost all gone. It was time to go home to his lonely cottage up the dusty track outside the village. His feet ached from all his walking and stalking, and he was hungry and thirsty.

When he saw the glint of the river ahead, he decided to stop for a rest and some food, thinking perhaps he might also bathe his weary feet. As he slithered down the path he saw a flash of movement by the river bank, and so he crept behind a great willow tree as quietly as possible. Perhaps it was some beast that had also stopped for a drink. The tree provided perfect cover for him as its weeping branches hung so low they trailed in the water. He peered through the leaves as, very stealthily, he fitted an arrow into his bow.

But the bow fell uselessly from his hands. It was no beast he was looking at, but three of the most beautiful maidens he had ever seen. They were wood nymphs. Their cloaks swirled round as they walked, rainbow colours reflected in the water. One was as dark as burnished walnut, one as fair as newly-fallen snow and the third glowed like the setting sun. Severe was utterly mesmerized. Time seemed to stand still as he gazed on the three exquisite nymphs and his heart beat so loudly he was sure they would hear.

They laughed and sang as they splashed about, filling a large earthenware flagon with the crystal-clear water from the river, quite unaware that someone was watching them. But then Severe moved a step closer and, in his distraction, stood on a twig which snapped with a loud crack. The three nymphs whirled round in fright, and caught sight of Severe. In a flash they were up and out of the water, and running through the wood as fast as frightened hares.

Severe scrambled after them, but they were faster by far and soon all he could see was an occasional flash of colour as they fled ever onwards, deeper into the wood. His breathing grew laboured, but still he ploughed on. As he stumbled into a clearing he realized he could see them no longer, but at the far side of the clearing stood three lovely trees, swaying gently in the breeze, their leaves trembling as if in fright. One was a waving ash, one a magnolia in full bloom and the third a glowing maple with golden leaves.

Severe knew the trees must be the beautiful maidens, and surely the maple was the nymph who glowed like the setting sun. He wrapped his arms round the trunk of the maple and tears rolled down his cheeks on to the smooth bark of the tree. From that moment on Severe lived in the woods, never returning to his lonely cottage up the dusty track outside the village.

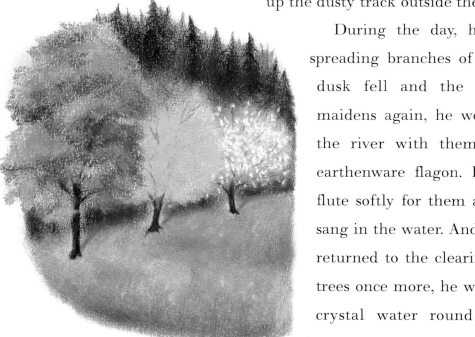

During the day, he slept under the spreading branches of the maple, but as dusk fell and the trees turned into maidens again, he would walk down to the river with them to fill the large earthenware flagon. He would play his flute softly for them as they danced and sang in the water. And when they had all returned to the clearing and turned into trees once more, he would pour the clear crystal water round their roots with infinite care. The nymphs came to trust and respect their gentle guardian.

He learned from the maple tree nymph that her name was Nephele, and, for all that she looked so young, she was in fact as old as the hills. Severe loved her with all his heart, and Nephele loved him too, but she always told him that she could never leave her sisters and come to live with him as a mortal.

Years passed, and still Nephele was young and beautiful and loved Severe, but he was growing old and tired. He longed to stop time so he might be with Nephele forever, but he realized that one day he must die and be parted from her. Nephele could not bear his sadness and so she called on the Goddess Diana to help them.

Diana was angry at first, for it was forbidden for nymphs and mortals to love each other. But her heart was touched by the care with which Severe looked after Nephele and her sisters, and she resolved to help the lovers. She took some water from the enchanted spring deep in the wood and gave it to Severe to drink, promising him that he and Nephele would be together until the end of time if he had the courage to drink the water without knowing what would happen to him. Nephele was frightened, for she knew the ways of the Gods, but Severe did not hesitate. He took the water from Diana and, tipping his head back, swallowed it in one long gulp.

Pain shot through his body. His neck seemed to be stretched to the point of breaking. He fell to his knees as his arms stiffened in their sockets.

A great plumed tail sprang from the base of his spine and a fine long twisted horn formed on his forehead. He became aware of all kinds of sounds and smells that he had never been aware of before, and he could hear what the birds in the trees were saying. He could hear the murmurings of hundreds of little creatures under the earth, and the whirring of the wings of the butterflies in the flowers. Nephele by his side, he moved slowly and walked down to the river where he gazed at his reflection in the still, calm water. He had become a unicorn. In his great joy he tossed his mane, stamped his golden hoofs and whinnied in sheer delight.

As light as a breath of wind, Nephele climbed up on to his smooth white back and together they galloped through the woods, she golden as the setting sun and he gleaming silver like the new moon. And they were together for all time, golden nymph and silver unicorn.

THE WHITE GANDER

OH, BUT SÉAMUS WAS A LAZY LUMP! His poor widowed mother worked her fingers to the bone on their little farm, milking the cows before the sun had risen, scattering corn for the hens, and drawing water from the well. Her son meanwhile snored away in bed, his head full of impossible dreams. Séamus fancied himself as a poet, and truth to tell, he could have been quite a good poet if he hadn't been so idle. It was the same with the uilleann pipes. His father had been a real master, famous throughout the county, but Séamus only knew the one tune. As luck would have it there was a great shortage of pipers, so despite his lack of skill Séamus was always asked to play at weddings and funerals.

It was Halloween, and Séamus lifted his pipes down off the wall.

'Mother,' he shouted, 'That's myself off to the dance down the valley.'

'You take care, Séamus,' said his mother. 'This is not a night to be out, the Púca will be riding the land.'

'Tush, Mother. I'm not scared of the old Púca,' said the foolish Séamus.

His mother crossed herself. The Púca was a mischievous spirit that looked like a small horse, but had two great horns curling up from its forehead. It was said to seek out its victims on Halloween.

'Better men than you have fallen foul of the Púca. So keep your wits about you and don't go drinking too much whiskey. And I'll have a freshly baked soda bread waiting for you when you return,' called his mother. There was a full moon that night, and the path lay ahead of him over the hills like a thread of silver ribbon. Séamus whistled the one tune he knew, and never noticed the dark shadow that crept behind him as he walked.

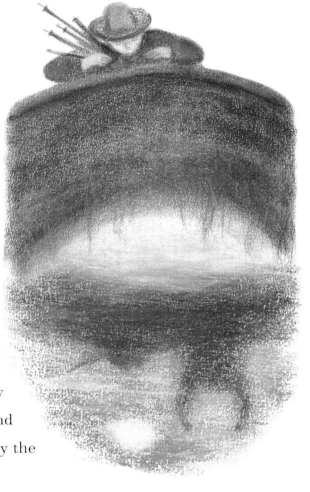

Before very long, and without mischance, Séamus reached the dance. Light blazed from the open door and a jar of whiskey was placed in his hand as soon as he stepped inside. Everyone was waiting for him, and no one minded that he had only the one tune as they reeled their way round the floor. All night long they danced and Séamus had emptied many jars of whiskey by the time it came to go home.

'Now you mind the Púca,' everyone laughed as he stepped outside once more, his pipes tucked under his arm, and made his way somewhat unsteadily down the road. No-one noticed the dark shadow that crept behind him once again. Séamus was very weary. He had no thought at all of the Púca, which was unwise as you shall see. All he could think of was his bed and his mother's soda bread waiting for him.

The road seemed never ending. Surely it was longer than when he had come down it earlier? When he reached the little bridge over the river he stopped to look down at the swirling black water. The moon wavered behind his head in the reflection, and with a thrill of terror Séamus saw that somebody, or rather, something, was standing behind him. He clutched his pipes closer and then he heard a sly voice in his ear.

'Can you play "The White Gander"?'

Séamus whirled round. There stood the Púca.

'Can you play "The White Gander"?' the Púca asked again.

Séamus spluttered. 'I don't think I know that one.'

'Well, it's time you did,' said the Púca. 'Come here and let me teach you.'

Séamus could not move a finger, never mind play the pipes, so terrified was he. The Púca moved closer, his horns glinting in the moonlight.

'Play,' he said again.

With his heart thumping so loudly that Séamus felt sure it would drown out the pipes, he began to play. Imagine his astonishment when the notes flew from his fingers and the air was filled with the most marvellous tune he had ever heard.

'Ah that's a grand tune to be sure,' said the Púca, 'I know who would like to hear that played. Come with me, and you will see what you will see.'

The Púca trotted off down the path and Séamus somehow found himself clutching his pipes and running after him as if his life depended on it, which it probably did at that moment. Over hills and through bogs, under spreading trees and across rivers, never once did the Púca hesitate, and somehow Séamus managed to keep up.

'Where are we going?' he managed to gasp.

'Ho, wouldn't you like to know!' laughed the Púca. 'Well, my bonny boy, we are going to Knocknashee, the fairy mountain. They are having a party too.' The Púca came to an abrupt halt in front of green

mound that rose up out of a wild bog. He knocked on the mound with his horns and a door swung open, silvery fairy light spilling on to the ground.

'Come away in,' whispered the Púca as he skipped down a long tunnel. Séamus followed, wondering what he was about to discover. The tunnel opened into a lofty hall, lit by

thousands of tiny candles. The floor glistened with golden leaves and heavy tapestries of silk hung from the walls. In the centre of the room was a long table laden with dishes of food and flagons of ruby red wine. But Séamus had no eyes for the food or the wine. He was transfixed by the figures sitting round the table.

They were hags, a hundred terrible, wrinkled, old hags. Never had Séamus seen people so ugly in all his life. Their hair was matted and tangled like dirty grey snakes. They had not a tooth between them, and their filthy hands ended in birds' talons. Their dresses were ragged and torn, and all were a dreary black. But when they saw Séamus they beamed at him.

'Ah and what have you brought for us tonight, Púca?' they shrieked.

'Nothing but the best for you ladies. Here is the best piper in all Ireland, and he is going to play for you!' said the Púca, shoving the reluctant Séamus forward. 'Give him something to eat and drink!'

But Séamus was not so daft as to eat any of the food that the hags offered him. Full well he knew that if you eat fairy food you are forever in their thrall. The hags saw they were not going to persuade their unwilling guest to partake of their splendid feast, but they were determined to get what they most wanted, the chance to reel and spin in the dance. A white gander walked in, carrying a chair which he set before Séamus.

'There you are, Séamus,' cried the hags, 'now you must play for us.'

And so Séamus began to play, and just as at the bridge, the notes flew from his fingers and the air was filled with the most marvellous tunes he had ever heard. The hags whirled and spun, dancing as though their very heels were on fire. On and on they danced, on and on Séamus played, as if devils were at his elbow. He played for hours it seemed, with never a break. His arms ached, his fingers flew and still the hags danced.

And then suddenly the white gander flapped up to Séamus and, before he realized what was happening, had pecked a great hole in the pipes. They wailed to a sudden stop and silence fell over the hall. Séamus took out his handkerchief and as he mopped his sweating face a sweet voice said,

'Well and isn't that a good thing now. If the white gander hadn't stopped you, sure and we would all be dead.'

There stood the most beautiful girl he had ever seen. And all around her stood beautiful girls. All the hags had vanished and there in their stead glowed a hundred fairy maidens. Their eyes were sparkling as they smiled at Séamus, their rainbow coloured skirts swirling as they moved.

'Thank you, Séamus. Your piping has made us young again,' said one of the fairy maidens. 'We are sorry about your father's pipes, but the white gander has another set for you. You will truly be the best piper in all of Ireland now!' And another maiden pressed a bag of gold coins into Séamus' hands, saying as she did,

'You must never tell anyone where these pipes came from, Séamus or the white gander will come and pierce them and you will never be able to play again.'

'One last thing, Séamus,' said all hundred maidens at once. 'YOU MUST BE KINDER TO YOUR MOTHER!'

Before he had a chance to open his mouth, Séamus found himself back on the bridge. In the distance a cock crowed. It was morning!

Séamus walked home, his new pipes tucked under his arm and the bag of gold clinking at every step. He stepped inside the cottage and there on the table was his mother's soda bread waiting for him. He sat down to eat a hearty breakfast, then he went outside and milked the cows, fed the hens and drew the water. Finally he took his astonished mother a cup of tea in bed.

When he had told her the story, she smiled at her foolish son.

'Well, now, perhaps you will listen to your old mother for a change! "I'm not scared of the old Púca" indeed!'

Séamus was indeed a changed man. He looked after his mother and did all the work on the farm so she could rest in her old age. He played the uilleann pipes the fairies had given him at all the weddings and dances in the valley and his fame spread throughout Ireland. He became most famous for the tune 'The White Gander' which no-one else seemed to know how to play. But he never, ever played it on Halloween!

INDEX

BIBLIOGRAPHY

Gods Men and Monsters Michael Gibson (Peter Lowe, 1977)

Great Swedish Fairy Tales Helger Lundbergh (Chatto and Windus, 1966)

The Dancing Fox John Bierhorst (William Morrow & Co, 1997)

History of Mythology Veronica Ions (Chancellor Press, 2000)

Heroes Monsters and Other Worlds Elizabeth Warner (Peter Lowe, 1985)

Irish Fairy Tales and Legends Una Leavy (The O'Brien Press, 1996)

Arabian Fairy Tales Amina Shah (The Octagon Press, 1989)

The Unicorn Nancy Hathaway (The Viking Press, 1980)

The Greek Myths Robert Graves (Penguin, 1992)